*To Katie Oz, who helped
with the words and may
someday do the pictures.*

TIM STAFFORD

John Porter in Big Trouble

ILLUSTRATIONS BY
Julie Park

A LION PICTURE STORY
Oxford · Batavia · Sydney

For his birthday, John Porter asked for a Powerman. His mother said no. 'You can play with a Powerman at other people's houses. But you cannot have one.'

'Why not?'

'Because Powermen are violent toys, and there is enough violence in the world without making up more.'

'It's not fair,' John said.

'Probably not,' his mother said.

'Timmy has two Powermen.'

'That may be so, but you are not Timmy. You are John Porter.'

Instead of a Powerman, John's parents gave him a set of coloured pencils. They were not just any ordinary coloured pencils. They were an artist's set of thirty-five pencils in every colour you can imagine.

John might have been very happy with the pencils but, when he opened them at the party, Timmy said, 'I thought you were going to get a Powerman!'

'Powerman is a bad toy,' John said. 'It is violent. They will probably make a law against them.'

But after the party John wished he had a Powerman. He used his pencils to draw Powermen. Big ones, little ones. Green ones, purple ones.

He drew a picture of a Powerman protecting Planet Earth from evil robots.

He drew another picture of Powermen fighting the War of the Submarines.

Most of these pictures he drew on his big pad of rainbow paper. However, one picture he drew on his mother's new wallpaper on the upstairs landing.

As soon as he had done it, he knew he was in trouble. He tried to erase it with the big eraser, but the colours did not come off.

He tried to cover it with a chair, but Powerman's head was too tall.

John Porter knew that if he could not hide the picture he would have to hide himself.

One time, after he had put the goldfish in the toilet, he had hidden under the bushes in Mr Shepherd's garden. But his father had seen his feet sticking out. John could not think of any hiding-place that his father would not see. His father had X-ray eyes.

The only way to hide from his father would be to turn invisible.

Or to change into somebody else.

That is why John Porter decided to change his name. From now on, John Porter decided, he would be somebody else.

He would be Daryl.

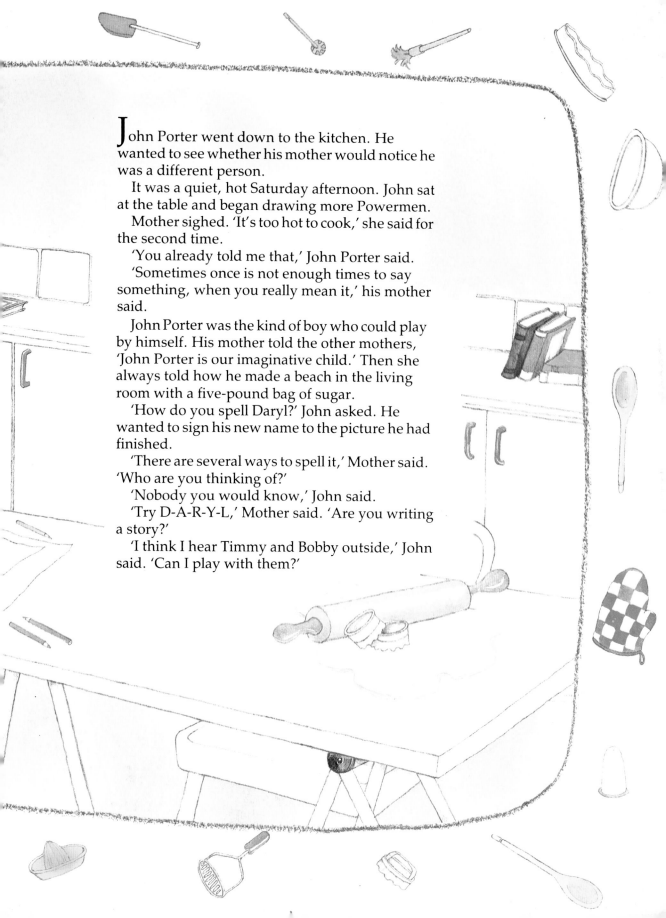

John Porter went down to the kitchen. He wanted to see whether his mother would notice he was a different person.

It was a quiet, hot Saturday afternoon. John sat at the table and began drawing more Powermen.

Mother sighed. 'It's too hot to cook,' she said for the second time.

'You already told me that,' John Porter said.

'Sometimes once is not enough times to say something, when you really mean it,' his mother said.

John Porter was the kind of boy who could play by himself. His mother told the other mothers, 'John Porter is our imaginative child.' Then she always told how he made a beach in the living room with a five-pound bag of sugar.

'How do you spell Daryl?' John asked. He wanted to sign his new name to the picture he had finished.

'There are several ways to spell it,' Mother said. 'Who are you thinking of?'

'Nobody you would know,' John said.

'Try D-A-R-Y-L,' Mother said. 'Are you writing a story?'

'I think I hear Timmy and Bobby outside,' John said. 'Can I play with them?'

John Porter went outside. There was no sign of Timmy or Bobby, so he went to their house and knocked on the door. He could see their father watching a game on TV.

'Can I play?' John asked.

'You have to play outside,' their father said. 'Timmy! Bobby!'

Timmy and Bobby came out. 'Hi, John,' they said together.

John said, 'I have a new name. From now on you should call me Daryl.'

'Uh oh. What did you do?' Timmy asked.

'Nothing,' John said. 'But if you see John Porter, tell him to be careful. He's in big trouble.'

'But you're John Porter,' Timmy said.

'Not any more. I changed my name to Daryl.'

Bobby thought about that. 'I don't think it will work,' he said.

'Sometimes spies get a new name,' John Porter said. 'They go to a foreign country and nobody knows they are spies.'

'But you can't go to a foreign country,' Timmy said. 'You have to go home.'

Just then John's father began to call for him. 'John! John Porter!' The way he sounded made John Porter wish he had hidden in the bushes.

'It isn't going to work,' Timmy said.

'I told you,' Bobby said.

'He is calling for John Porter,' John said. 'If you see him, make sure you tell him my father is looking for him.'

They heard the sound of John Porter's door slamming.

'I knew it wouldn't work,' Timmy said.

'I told you,' Bobby said.

John Porter's father did not say anything. He took John's hand and led him inside the house, to the landing on the second floor. 'What do you see?' he asked.

'Mum's new wallpaper,' John said. 'She did a good job.'

'Do you see anything else?'

'It looks as if someone drew a picture. Not really very good.'

'Anything else?' Father asked. 'Did the artist sign his work, for instance?'

'There is a name at the bottom.'

'Can you read it?'

'It says John Porter.'

'Do you know what that means?'

'It means John Porter is really going to be in trouble.'

'That's right,' said Father. 'You are in trouble.'

'Not me, Dad,' said John Porter. 'My name is Daryl. If I see John, I will tell him he is in big trouble.'

Father looked at John Porter. 'Daryl?' he said.

'Yes.'

'Since when are you Daryl?'

'Oh, my name has been Daryl for as long as I remember.'

'You probably don't remember very long,' Father said. 'You probably can't remember whether you drew a picture on your mother's new wallpaper. So why don't you go to your room, and when you are able to remember you may come out and apologize to your mother, and we will think about what to do next.'

John Porter sat on his bed. He could hear his mother and father talking with his little brother downstairs, but he could not hear what they were saying. He opened the door and put his head outside, but he still could not hear.

'Can I come out now?' he called down the stairs.

'Are you ready to say you're sorry?' his father called up the stairs.

'It is very boring in my room,' John said. 'There is nothing to do.'

'Good,' his father said. 'That will keep you from getting into more trouble. Now get back in your room before I come up the stairs.'

John went back into his room. He looked in his cupboard, where all his games were stacked up. He looked on his shelves, where he kept his art materials.

Everything was boring.

John Porter sat down on his bed and cried. Then he stopped and listened. Then he cried some more.

'I could hear you the first time,' his mother said from just outside his door. 'When you are ready to say sorry, you may come out.'

John could hear Timmy and Bobby playing in the sprinkler. They were having fun.

'I am not having fun,' John Porter said to himself, out loud. 'It is not fun to be someone you are not. Especially if your father and mother are cross with you.'

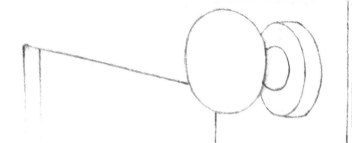

John opened his door. His mother was on the landing with a bucket and a sponge. She was cleaning the picture off the wallpaper.

'Is it coming off?' he asked.

'A little,' she said. 'I need some help. Are you ready to say you are sorry?'

'I am dying of thirst.'

'I will bring you a glass of water, then,' Mother said. She got up.

'That's all right,' John said. 'I am not so thirsty. I am sorry that I drew on the wall.'

John helped his mother clean the picture off the wallpaper. The blue and red pencil came off easily, but the yellow was hard.

'Mum?' John said.

'Yes, John?'

'Did you think it was a good picture?'

'It was a terrific picture. Just in the wrong place.'

That night, when it was story time, John asked if they could read from the red book his aunt had given him for Christmas.

'You mean the picture story Bible?' his father asked.

'Yes. Could we read about the first man and the first woman?'

John and his father sat on the sofa, reading about how Adam and Eve and all the animals were made. John's mother and little brother Tom listened. The book had a picture of Adam stroking a baby zebra, and Eve holding a baby lion. When they had finished reading, John's father stood up to put the book away.

'Isn't there more?' John asked. So John's father read the next story, about how Adam and Eve disobeyed God and tried to hide. The book had a picture of them crouching in the bushes.

'Is that what you wanted?' John's father asked. John nodded yes.

'Do you think they didn't have a very good hiding place?' John asked.

'Why do you say that?' John's father answered.

'Because God found them straight away. Maybe they were such new people they didn't know how to hide.'

John's father laughed. 'Maybe they didn't. But anyway, I don't think people can hide from God. He can always find them, even if they choose a very good hiding place.'

Father said, 'Now I have a question for you. What did you mean when you said your name was Daryl?'

John was embarrassed. He put his head down into his lap and looked at his knees. 'I wanted to hide from you because I knew I was in trouble.'

Father put his hand on John's arm. It felt warm and firm there. His voice sounded happy. 'John Porter, did you think you could hide from me by pretending to be somebody else?'

John did not answer.

'John Porter, when you were just a little tiny baby your mother and I gave you your name. We love you. And John Porter is your name, no matter what you call yourself. Other people may not know who you are, but we always will. You can never hide from your father. Or your mother, either.'

16

John Porter lifted up his head. He had tears in his eyes. He leaned over, across the sofa, and gave his mother a big hug.

'John Porter, what goes on in your head?' Mother asked. 'No matter what name you call yourself, we will always know who you are. We gave you your name. We love you.'

'You already told me that,' John said.

'Sometimes once is not enough times to say something, when you really mean it,' his mother said.

Text copyright © 1990 Tim Stafford
Illustrations copyright © 1990 Julie Park

Published by
Lion Publishing plc
Sandy Lane West, Oxford, England
ISBN 0 7459 2257 0
Albatross Books Pty Ltd
PO Box 320, Sutherland, NSW 2232, Australia
ISBN 0 7324 0560 2

First edition 1990
First paperback edition 1993

A catalogue record for this book is available
from the British Library

Printed and bound in Singapore

Other picture storybooks in paperback from Lion Publishing

Albert Blows A Fuse Tom Bower
Baboushka Arthur Scholey
The Donkey's Day Out Ann Pilling
The Lark Who Had No Song Carolyn Nystrom
A Lion for the King Meryl Doney
Mabel and the Tower of Babel John Ryan
Papa Panov's Special Day Mig Holder
Roberto and the Magical Fountain Donna Reid Vann
Stefan's Secret Fear Donna Reid Vann
The Tale of Three Trees Angela Elwell Hunt
The Very Worried Sparrow Meryl Doney